Tales from Parc la Fontaine

Written and Illustrated
by Roslyn Schwartz

Annick Press

TORONTO · NEW YORK · VANCOUVER

Trevor and the French Fry

It was a day like any other when Trevor decided to escape ...

to take a walk in Parc la Fontaine …

to act wild.

WHEEEEE

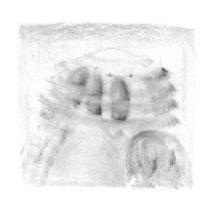

WAAAGH

WIGGLE WIGGLE

"Hello, Trevor," said Willie.

"Sssh! Don't speak to me,"
said Trevor.

"I'm acting wild."

"What's that?"

SPLAT

"It's a french fry!"   "Mmmm, yummy."

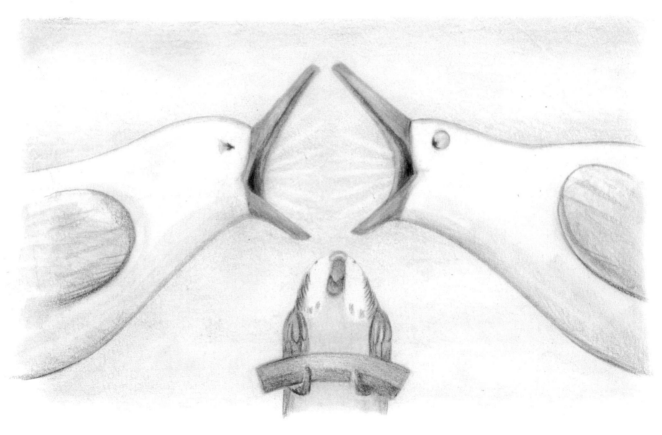

"I saw it first!"   "No, I saw it first!"

"Hey hey hey"

"I saw it first."

"It was mine."

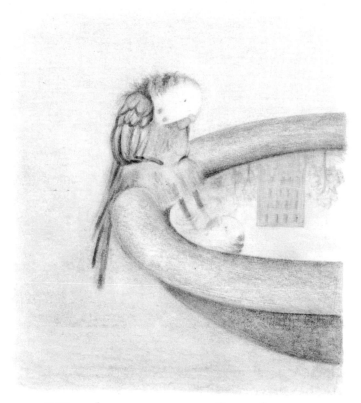

"I'm hungry, my feet hurt,
and I'm tired of acting wild."

"I know what,"
said Trevor.

"I'm going home now, Willie."

"Bye, Trevor," said Willie.
"See you next week."

"Mmmm," said Trevor.

The End

Fiona the Lonely Land Snail

Fiona the lonely land snail was on a quest
for true everlasting love.

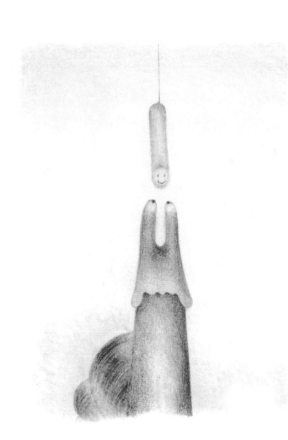

"Hello, Fiona."

"Oh, hello, Colin."

"Who's that?"

CHOMP CHOMP
CHEW CHEW

"It's a baby caterpillar."

"Isn't he adorable?"

"Yes but, Fiona," said Colin, "he's a baby caterpillar
and we know what that means."

"It'll end in tears."

"I know," said Fiona, "but I can't help it – he's so cute!"

"Every year Fiona falls in love with a baby caterpillar."

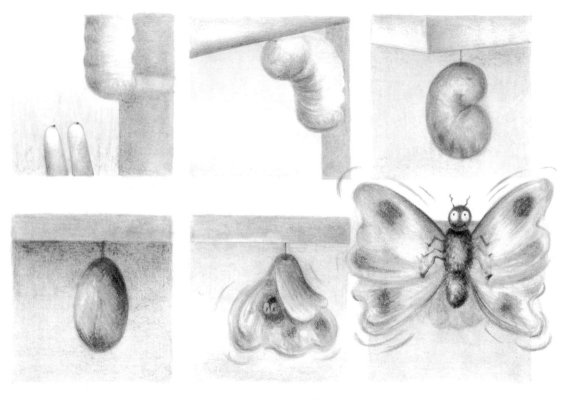

"And every year the baby caterpillar turns into a butterfly
and the butterfly …"

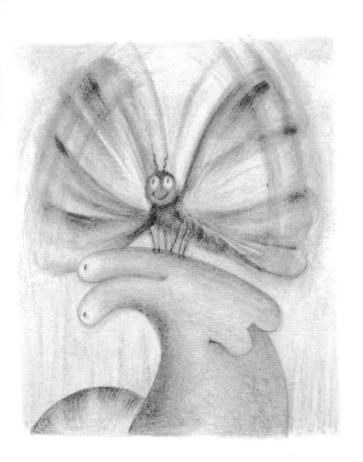

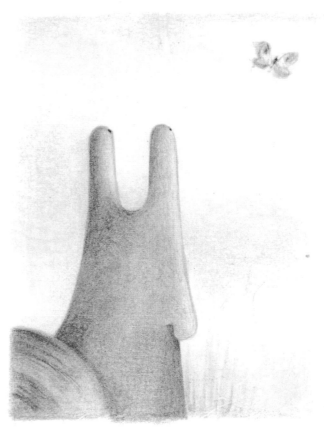

FLIT FLIT   FLUTTER FLUTTER

"flies away."

"Cheer up, Fiona."

"It looks like rain."

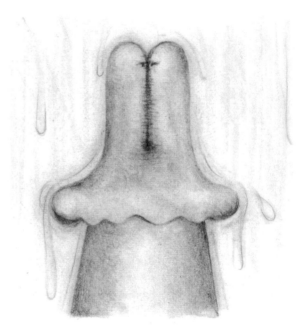

"Rain!" said Fiona.

"Oh goodie, I love the rain.
It makes me slimy all over."

And Fiona forgot all about baby caterpillars ...
'til the next time.

The End

Angela's Day

Angela had but one life to live.   And one day to live it in.

"First things first," said Angela ...

PLOINK PLOINK

and she laid a big pile of eggs.

Everyone was very impressed.

Whatever next?

"I don't know," said Angela, "but I'm going to find out."

BUZZ BUZZ   **SNAP SNAP**

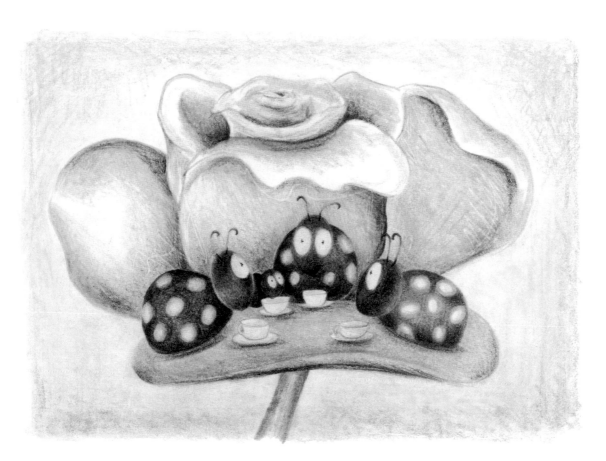

NATTER NATTER

TSK TSK   GUZZLE GUZZLE

SHOO SHOO

THERE THERE

BEEP BEEP

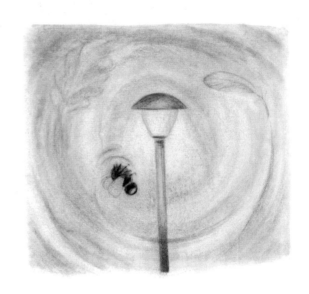

WHOOOOSH

HOORAH
"I did it," said Angela.

TWINKLE TWINKLE

"I lived my whole life in just one day."

The End

We acknowledge the support of the Canada Council for the Arts, the Ontario Arts
Council, and the Government of Canada through the Book Publishing Industry
Development Program (BPIDP) for our publishing activities.

Cataloging in Publication Data

Schwartz, Roslyn, 1951-
        Tales from Parc la Fontaine / written and illustrated by Roslyn Schwartz.

(The Parc la Fontaine series)
ISBN-13: 978-1-55451-044-3 (bound)
ISBN-13: 978-1-55451-043-6 (pbk.)
ISBN-10: 1-55451-044-9 (bound)
ISBN-10: 1-55451-043-0 (pbk.)

        I. Title. II. Series: Schwartz, Roslyn, 1951- Parc la Fontaine series.

PS8587.C5785T34 2006   jC813'.54   C2006-900830-2

The art in this book was rendered in coloured pencils.
The text was typeset in Edwardian Script and Bodoni.

Distributed in Canada by: Published in the U.S.A.
Firefly Books Ltd.   by Annick Press (U.S.) Ltd.
66 Leek Crescent   Distributed in the U.S.A. by:
Richmond Hill, ON   Firefly Books (U.S.) Inc.
L4B 1H1   P.O. Box 1338
                                Ellicott Station
                                Buffalo, NY 14205

Printed and bound in China.

visit us at: **www.annickpress.com**